John Ross Macduff, Anna Elizabeth Hamilton, Edith S. Jacob

Comfort for Hours of Sorrow

John Ross Macduff, Anna Elizabeth Hamilton, Edith S. Jacob

Comfort for Hours of Sorrow

ISBN/EAN: 9783337780524

Printed in Europe, USA, Canada, Australia, Japan

Cover: Foto ©Andreas Hilbeck / pixelio.de

More available books at **www.hansebooks.com**

COMFORT FOR HOURS OF SORROW

Even here,
From His dear children's eyes, God wipes the tear;
And who would mourn, a tear should fill his eye
For God to dry!
Angels might envy man his tearful eyes
When God's hand dries.

A. E. H.

NEW YORK
E. P. DUTTON AND COMPANY
713 BROADWAY

NOTE.

THE *Poems* in this book are by *Miss A. E. Hamilton*, a gifted young Irish lady who has lately died.

"*The First Bereavement*" is by the Rev. J. R. Macduff, D. D., well known as the Author of "The Faithful Promiser," "Words and Mind of Jesus," etc., etc.

"*The Gate of Paradise*" is anonymous, but has been received with much favor both in England and in this country. The compiler trusts that the whole may be acceptable and soothing to many afflicted ones, when the sacredness of sorrow forbids other communion.

THE CHRISTIAN MOURNER.

1.

I THANK Thee for this heavy loss ;
I thank Thee for this bitter cross;
Because it hath seemed good to Thee,
To send this cross and loss to me.

2.

I know it was no random blow
Which laid thee, my own darling, low;
Not death, but Christ, who said to thee
" Come hither, oh! my friend, to me."

3.

Death hides, but he cannot divide ;
Thou art but on Christ's other side ;
Thou art with Christ, and Christ with me,
In Christ united still are we.

4.

I know that Christ will never chide
My sorrow, He hath wept and sighed ;
I feel the pressure of His hand,
I know that He doth understand.

5.

And oh ! what blessedness, relief,
To tell the Christ of God my grief ;
Dear Man of Sorrows, Thou art still
The refuge for all human ill.

6.

And Thou wilt still be more to me,
For that dear one who is with Thee ;
Thus Thou wilt fill the vacant place
In Thy deep tenderness and grace.

DEATH AND THE JEWELS.

I.

" I AM no thief," quoth Death, " I only bor-
    row
  The treasures that I take from thee to-
    day ;
Christ will restore thee fourfold on the mor-
    row ;
  For when He comes again, He will re-
    pay."

2.

I looked at Death, my heart beat loud and
    faster :
  " In loan for Christ these treasures I re-
    ceive ;
I am the faithful servant of thy Master ;
  Doubt not," he said, " but earnestly be-
    lieve."

3.

" Knowest thou," I cried, "that these are all
    my pleasures,
    Which thou art bearing to the far-off land?"
As I reluctantly beheld my treasures
    Shining like pearls in his dim orient hand.

4.

"Fear not," he said, as from my sight he
    slowly
    Vanished, the sunlight on his raven wings.
Making them shine, half awful and half holy;
    "These are the jewels of the King of kings."

5.

" These are His jewels, and to Him I bear
    them,
    To deck His robes of immortality;
These are thy treasures, and the Christ will
    wear them,
    That where thy treasures are thy heart may
    be."

THE UNSEEN.

1.

WE walk beneath the shelter of God's wings,
While by our pathway Hope, His angel, sings
Of the unseen and everlasting things.

2.

She sings to us of Heaven, the great Home-
    land,
And our eternal house, "not made with hand,"
Preparing for us there by Christ's command.

3.

That not as strangers shall we reach its shore,
Friendless, an unknown region to explore;
Our Elder Brother hath gone on before.

4.

And of the wondrous Resurrection hour,
When from the dust of earth each buried flower
Shall come forth, clothed with glory, honor,
    power.

AFFLICTIONS.

As a ploughed field,
Left desolate and bare
To winter storms and chilly, frosty air,
Yet only thus made dreary for a while,
That richer there the harvest grain may smile;
So is the heart whose sod,
Tender and green,
Hath been
Upturned by God,
Its sprouting blades laid low;
Yet only broken thus by grief's ploughshare,
That in its furrows He might sow
The seed of righteousness which shall increase
Until it yield the harvest of eternal peace.

BEREAVEMENT.

1.

WHEN we behold
God walking through our household fold,
And choosing there one of His own dear
sheep,
Whom we would keep,
How can our eyes forbear to weep?

2.

Where God doth ask,
Is it to give so hard a task?
That with so much ado and weeping,
We yield to His eternal keeping?
Where He hath sown, can we forbid the
reaping?

3.

Take, then, the best,
Fold them as lambs within Thy breast,
And with Thy Holy Spirit's dew,
So, blessed Lord, our hearts renew,
That we some day be folded by Thee too.

SORROW.

SHOULD Sorrow lay her hand upon thy shoul-
    der,
  And walk with thee in silence on life's way,
While Joy, thy bright companion once, grown
    colder,
  Becomes to thee more distant day by day?
Shrink not from the companionship of Sor-
    row,
  She is the messenger of God to thee;
And thou wilt thank Him in His great to-
    morrow—
  For what thou knowest not now, thou then
    shalt see:
She is God's angel, clad in weeds of night,
With "whom we walk by faith and not by
    sight."

THANKFULNESS.

1.

AND when life seemed a blank,
And all thy heart within thee sank,
· Couldst thou thy God still thank?

2.

Even as Christ above the wine and bread,
Emblems to Him of agony and dread,
Thanked God His blood for sinners should
    be shed.

3.

Then bless thy God in all such pain and
    loss,
For teaching thee the lessons of the Cross;
The hardest stone He covers with His moss.

DEATH DESPOILED.

Ezekiel xxxiv. 11, 12.

I HAD a vision of Death passing by
Crowned:
His victims scattered round did lie.
I shuddering fell upon the ground.
When, lo! a shout of victory,
Aroused me from despair profound.
I hasten'd to my door,
And saw Death passing by,
Once more,
But bound
And captive led
By One arisen from the dead.

THE RESURRECTION.

REV. i. 18.

AND dost thou marvel that He should arise
Who opened death-closed eyes?
Wouldst thou not rather marvel if the tomb
  Could him retain
In its dark gloom,
  Who did for others loose its pain?
He did therein consent three days to lie
To comfort us who die,
That for His sake
We, too, might also slumber and awake.

"THE FORM OF THE FOURTH IS LIKE THE SON OF GOD."

DANIEL iii. 25.

O SON OF GOD! Thy form is ever found
Where'er the sufferings of Thy saints abound:
In fiery furnace or on midnight sea
They walk with Thee;
And in the charm
Of thy supporting arm
Forget the winds and waves or fiery flames
around.

THE

FIRST BEREAVEMENT:

OR

WORDS ADDRESSED TO A MOURNER ON
THE OCCASION OF A FIRST TRIAL.

By L. R. Macduff, d.d.

THIS is a solemn hour on which you have entered. The shadows of death for the first time are falling around your dwelling. Often before have you heard of trial. You may have visited over and over again the house of affliction. You may even have dealt out lessons of comfort to others. The doors of neighbours and friends

you have seen darkened with bereavement, but the King of Terrors has till now passed you by.
Your turn has at last come!—
The spoiler has broken into your
fond circle. The gourd is withered, the "beautiful rod" has been
broken. Your heart is smitten like
grass. For the first time yours is
a house of death,—yours the bitterness of a *First Bereavement.**

By the help of Him who is the
healer of the broken-hearted I
would desire to pour some drops
of consolation into your wound-

---

* "Ah, what lessons our dear Lord is now
teaching you, lessons which angels can never
learn;—teaching by heart what was only known
before by rote!"— *Lady Powerscourt's Letters.*

ed bosom. This little book is intended to be seen by no eyes but weeping ones. It addresses no hearts but broken ones. It is to speak of sorrows with which a stranger cannot intermeddle. The world at such a time is often unwilling to make allowances for the sacredness of grief. He who wept at the grave of Bethany puts no such, unkind arrest on the outflowings of sorrow. He "wept with those that wept." He has told us to "go and do likewise."

I know not what this your first lesson in the school of Bereavement is. It may be "the desire of your eyes taken away by a

stroke." It may be a beloved
wife or husband, the sharer of
your every joy and sorrow, suddenly and mysteriously removed,
and you are left to shed the tears
of disconsolate widowhood. It
may be some fond parent, whose
smile gladdens and hallows every
memory of the past, and now you
find yourself treading orphaned
and alone the remainder of the
pilgrimage. It may be some darling child, who has imperceptibly
been entwining its every heart-
string around you, wrenched from
your embrace—a little light ex-
tinguished in your dwelling—the
favourite star of the firmament
quenched in the darkness of death;

one of those whose names are touchingly described as " always on grave-stones ; and their sweet smiles, their heavenly eyes, their singular words and ways, among the buried treasure of yearning hearts. In how many families do you hear the legend, that all the goodness and graces of the living are nothing to the peculiar charms of *one who is not !*"

Added to all this, the trial may have come with appalling suddenness. The hurricane may have swept your loved one down in the midst of brightest sunshine. Yesterday all was joyous and happy; to-day you are hurled by one

terrible blow from the pinnacles
of earthly bliss. Seated amid the
wreck and ruin of all that on earth
was held dear,—poor, lonely, desolate, you can say, with the touch-
ing emphasis of the broken-hearted Patriarch, "I AM bereaved!"
The yoke, too, may have been
early put upon your neck, or the
summons may have come at the
time when the joy of your heart
could be least spared; when most
prized, most needed, most loved!
It may have been some cherished
flower, rich with future promise,
which has in a night drooped and
withered and fallen; or some life
of signal usefulness to the church
or the world. Ten thousand with-

ered sapless trunks in the forest left untouched by the axe; the freshest and strongest and greenest marked out first to fall!

What! can it be? Is it indeed a sober truth? a sad reality? Or may it not prove some wild dream, some feverish vision which the night will dispel? Will not the morning chase away these terrible pictures of untold desolation? Alas! the morning comes, but with it the waking up only to a more vivid consciousness that all is too painfully real. These grey tints of early dawn are falling on a silent grave! "Joseph is not and Simeon is not." With the droop-

ing and blighting of that cherished gourd,

> " There's not on earth the living thing
> To which the withered heart can cling."

How strange and thrilling are
the feelings with which you find
yourself now amid the world's
familiar din and bustle ! The
unsympathizing crowd, all unconscious of what is transacting within your threshold, are hurrying
by as before. They are exchang-
ing with one another the same
joyous smiles, they are clad in
the same gay attire, the same
merry chimes mark the passing
hour, the same "ringing laugh of
childhood" is heard in the streets;

and yet to you, all is sicklied over with inveterate sadness ; every scene and association which whispers joy to others, reads but a homily of sorrow to your aching heart. You now can well understand words in the vocabulary of sorrow which once seemed strange — " *Wilderness world,*" " *Valley of tears.*" How call this world, you were once led to ask, " *wilderness* " and " *tearful,*" which is sparkling on every side with tints of loveliness and vocal with joy ? Right well do you know it *now !* Every flower has faded on your path. The silent chamber !— it echoes to your lonely voice. The happy fireside circle !

— there is a vacant seat. The
favourite walk, — the cherished
haunt! — the smile that made it
so is fled. Ah! life has indeed
become like the "flat, bare, oozy
tide-mud, when the blue sparkling
wave, with all its company of
gliding boats and white-winged
ships, the music of oars and chim-
ing waters, has gone down." Mate-
rial nature itself, the earth around
you, the very firmament above
you, seem to have shared in some
terrible catastrophe, as if wan and
coloured with ashes. You breathe
a different air, you are lighted by
a different sun; in one terrible
sense is the Scripture saying ex-
pounded, " old things have passed

away, and all things have become new."*

Reader, I can imagine you now, solitary and alone in your chamber, your eye dim with weeping; your mind filled with ten thousand conflicting feelings to which you dare not give utterance; the holy visions of the past flitting

* "As an iceberg comes grinding between two ships, sailing joyfully in company, so death rises up between these hearts, parting them for ever. The man awakes alone! and lo! the strength of his soul is departed! Nature is silent. For him the sun shines not; the beauty and grandeur of nature exist only as light to the blind and music to the deaf. The whole world of nature, art, poetry, music, painting, all are buried for him in that one grave." — *Shadows on the Hebrew Mountains. Mrs. Stowe.*

before you like shadows on the wall; the future all darkness and mystery.—Your pining heart in the first gush of its bitterness turns away, refusing to be comforted; the feelings of an old sufferer are too truthfully the transcript of your own, "Call me not Naomi, call me Mara, for the Almighty hath dealt very bitterly with me." (Ruth i. 20.) You may be even unable at first to get any comfort at the mercy-seat. You seek in vain to buffet the surges of grief; there is no light in the darkness, no break in the cloud, — "deep is calling unto deep."

Be comforted! "The Lord *will* command his loving-kindness in the day-time, and in the night his song shall be with me, and my prayer to the God of my life." Yes! "O thou afflicted, tossed with tempest and not comforted," unschooled and undisciplined in these fiery trials;—He who brought you into the furnace will lead you through! He has never failed in the case of any of His "poor afflicted ones" to realize His own precious promise, "As thy day is, so shall thy strength be." All is mystery and enigma to you *now*,—nothing but crossed plans, and blighted hopes, and a future of unutterable desolation.

But He will yet vindicate His dealings. I believe even on earth He often leads us to see and learn "the need be;" and if *not* on earth, at least in glory, there will be a grand revelation of ineffable wisdom and love in this very trial which is now bowing your head like a bulrush, and making your eyes a very fountain of tears.*

* "He is in all providences, be they never so bitter, never so afflicting, never so smarting, never so destructive to our earthly comforts. Christ is in them all; His love, His wisdom, His mercy, His pity, and compassion is in them all, every cup is of His preparing; it is Jesus, your best friend, (O ye poor, poor believers,) who most dearly loves you, that appoints all providences, orders them all, overrules, moderates, and sanctifies them all, and will sweeten them all, and in His due time will make them profitable unto you, that

But though I have dwelt on the depth of your bereavement, I do not write to make more tears to flow. My design is rather to dry them; — to mitigate these aching pangs, and lead you submissively to say, " Thy will be done." It is not a time when the mind is able or disposed to follow pages of continuous thought. Let me only throw out one or two simple reflections for your meditation, which I pray the Ho-

you shall one day have cause to praise and bless His name for them all. Oh that we could but believe all this, and could by faith look unto our Jesus in all dark providences, and by faith behold this Jesus managing of them, and believe His love, wisdom, tenderness, and faithfulness in all." — *Bunyan's Heart's Ease.*

ly Ghost the Comforter to bring
home to you. "May the Father
of mercies and God of all comfort,
who comforteth us in all our trib-
ulations," make us able to "comfort them which are in any trou-
ble, by the comfort wherewith
we ourselves are comforted of
God." (2 Cor. i. 3, 4.)

A First Trial! — *Was it not
needed?* Has not the world been
becoming too much for you; —
engrossing your affections, alien-
ating your love, dimming your
view of "the better country"?
Ah! commune with your own
heart, and say, was not this (terrible though it be) the *very disci-*

pline required? *Less* would not
have done, to wean me from the
poor nothings of earth. I was
lulled in a guilty self-security.
I was living in a state of awful
forgetfulness of my God, — insen-
sible of His mercies, — unmind-
ful of His goodness, — taking my
blessings as matters of course,
— a *secret atheism!* And, more
than this, of the awful magni-
tude of "things not seen" I had
no vivid consciousness. I felt
as if surely death could never
disturb my dream of happiness.
He had been going his rounds on
every side, but I never could realize the time when the terrible in-
vader could rush upon my loved

circle and make such *a gap as
this !*

Dear Reader! if such be aught
of a truthful picture, I ask you,
was it not *kindness, unspeakable
kindness* in thy covenant God to
break (though with a voice of
thunder) this perilous dream?—
to bring back "by terrible things
in righteousness" thy truant, wan-
dering, treacherous heart, and fix
once more thy traitor affections
on Himself as their only satisfy-
ing portion? "Your Heavenly
Father never thought this world's
painted glory a gift worthy of
you, and therefore He hath taken
out the best thing it had in your

sight that He might Himself fill the heart He had wounded *with* Himself." *

The threads of life were weaved into too bright a tissue, God had to snap them! — The loved one thou art now mourning was a *clay idol*, He had to break it in pieces. He had to drag it from the usurped throne that He might resume that throne Himself. He gave thee prosperity — but thou couldst not or *wouldst* not use it for His glory. It was a curse to thee! It was that awful thing, " unsanctified prosperity." Thou wert living on the borders of

* *Evans.*

that terrible state — " because they have no changes, therefore they fear not God." He would not suffer thee to be left alone, to settle in the downy nest of self-ease and forgetfulness. He has roused thee on the wing, and pointed thy upward soarings to their only true resting-place, in His own everlasting presence, and friendship, and love. "Ah! it is indeed humiliating," says the same holy man whose words we have last quoted, "that we require so many stripes to *force* us, as it were, to God, when there is enough in Him to draw us to Himself, and to keep us with Himself for ever!"   But better surely all these stripes than to be left unchecked in our career of forgetfulness. It has been well said, "the sorest word God ever spoke to Israel was, 'Why should ye be stricken any more?'" This wayward heart was throwing out its fibres on every side and rooting them down to earth. He had to unroot them!—to wrench these grovelling affections from the things that are of "earth, earthy," and fasten them on Himself as their all in all! *

* "How great a mercy," writes Richard Baxter to a tried friend, "was it to live thirty-eight years under God's wholesome discipline! O my God! I thank Thee for the like discipline of fifty-eight years! How safe is this in comparison of full prosperity and pleasure!"

A First Trial! *Was there not
graciousness in it?* At first sight
this may appear a strange ad-
mission to demand. There may
seem no star in that black sky,
no alleviating drop in the bitter,
bitter cup. But see that you
give not way to guilty murmurings, lest a worse thing come
upon you;—lest God may show
you "greater things than these!"
Pause and ask, have there been
in your affliction no mitigating
circumstances, no gracious consolations, "no tempering of the
wind to the shorn lamb," no "stay-
ing of His rough wind in the day
of His east wind"? "Have you
ever marked," says a writer who

knew well herself what the furnace was,—"have you ever marked His gentleness when bringing a painful message? how He usually calls by name, 'Abraham, Abraham!' 'Moses, Moses'?"*

Yes! I verily believe that there are few afflicted children of God but can echo the expression of the tried Psalmist, "I will sing of *mercy* and of judgment." (Mercy first, then judgment!) I ask you in this hour to think of your *mercies*, and let each of them be a voice of comfort to you. What are they? Have there been kind friends sent to share the bitterness

* *Lady Powerscourt's Letters.*

of your sorrow and give you the
tribute of their valued sympathy?
Ask those who, from peculiar circumstances, may have been de-
nied this boon; — who in their
hour of trial have been left unbefriended to weep in silence and
in solitude their first tears — ask
them, Is there no mercy in this?
Again, your *chief* blessing may
have been snatched away from
you, but many precious ties yet
remain ; and you will find, as
one most blessed and endearing
element in the loss you have
sustained, that it knits together
the broken links in holier and
more sacred bonds than before.
Ask those who have carried their

all to the grave—who have been left like a solitary tree of the forest *alone!*— all around them swept down!—ask *them*, if it be no blessing to have the cherished voice of doubly-endeared survivors to mingle together common tears, and recount the hallowed memories of the departed? Or, better than all, Is the loss you mourn the eternal gain of the absent one? Oh! ask those who have to muse in dumb agony over the thought of those gone unprepared to meet their God, ask *them*, Is it no small mercy, (nay, rather is it not the highest and most exalted of all consolations, — that which disarms

death and bereavement of all its
bitterness,—) that "the loved and
lost" are the crowned and glorified? "We may not here below,"
says St. Cyprian, "put on dark
robes of mourning, when they
above have put on the white
robes of glory." Does not this
hush all murmurs and dry all
tears, that the great end of their
being has been faithfully fulfilled?
"The birds are fled away, having
outgrown our care, to fill a bough
on the tree of life, and charm us
on to follow after them."

> " She is not dead, the child of our affection,
>   But gone into that school
>   Where she no longer needs our poor protec-
>   tion,
>   But Christ Himself doth rule.

In that great cloister's stillness and seclu-
    sion,
  By guardian angels led,
Safe from temptation, safe from sin's pollu-
    tion,
  She *lives* whom we call *dead*." *

* " I have had six children, and I bless
God for his free grace that they are all *with*
Christ, or *in* Christ, and my mind is now at
rest concerning them. My desire was that
they should have served Christ on earth,
but if God will choose to have them rather
serve Him in heaven, I have nothing to ob-
ject to it; His will be done." — *Elliot.*

" Let me be thankful for the pleasing hope,
that though God loves my child too well to
permit it to return to me, He will ere long
bring me to it, and then that endeared pater-
nal affection which would have been a cord
to tie me to earth, and have added new
pangs to my removal from it, will be as a
golden chain to draw me upwards, and add
one further charm and joy even to Paradise
itself. Was this my desolation, this my sorrow, to part with thee for a few days, that

THE FIRST TRIAL! *Is there not a specially loud Voice in it?* Yes!

I might receive thee for ever, (*Philemon* 15,) and find thee what thou art? It is for no language but that of heaven to describe the sacred joy which such a meeting must occasion." — *Philip Doddridge.*

We are told of Luther's daughter, " She expired, and as it were fell asleep, in the arms of her father. He repeated often, The will of God be done, my daughter has still. a Father in heaven." And when the people came to assist in bearing out the body, and, according to the common custom, told him that they shared his affliction, he said to them, " Be not troubled, I have sent a saint to heaven. Oh could we have such a death — *such a death,* I could accept it this hour."

"All our dear relations that died in Christ are triumphantly singing hallelujahs in the highest heavens. While we are fighting, sighing, and sobbing here below, they are with blessed Jesus above, according to His prayer for them, seeing His glory and participating in it." — *John Bunyan.*

I say so with a solemn convic-
tion of its truth — You *may* have
heavier trials and severer losses
than this, but never will God's
voice speak louder to you than
now. *It is the loudest knock that
can be heard at the door of your
heart!* Felix might have heard
another (perhaps even a more
powerful) sermon from Paul "on
righteousness, temperance, and the
judgment to come," but I believe
he would not have again trembled, as he did, when for THE FIRST
time these appalling realities were
presented to his mind.

A first trial, then, has its solemn
responsibilities! Let it not die

away, like the subsiding thunder, unsanctified and unimprov-
ed. Let it be accompanied with
the trembling response — "Lord,
what wouldst thou have me to
do?" Seek to feel that God has
thereby some great end in view
—some wise meaning to subserve
—some gracious lesson to teach.
Inquire what it is. Depend upon
it, your mind will never be in a
more impressible state than *now.*
Afflictions, like other voices, if
unheeded, only harden and ren-
der callous. Let the present be
regarded as the most solemn messenger you ever *can* hear, pro-
claiming, *"Prepare to meet thy
God."* It may be now or never

with you! Feel as if this bereavement were some gracious pre-
cursor sent to give you the time-
ly warning, "Be ye also ready!"
The first "pin taken from your
earthly tabernacle!"—Let it be as
a monitory angel telling you to
strike your tent and pitch it nearer heaven;—"Arise and depart,
for this is *not* your rest!" As
we have seen the timid bird hop-
ping from bough to bough till it
reach the topmost branch, and
then winging its flight to the
sky; so with the soul—affliction is designed to drive it from
bough to bough, from refuge to
refuge, higher and still higher,

till at last it soars upward to the Heaven of its God.*

THE FIRST TRIAL. *Is it not a befitting*, THE *most befitting season to give yourself unreservedly to the service of God?* Your hold is loosened from the world. Like a vessel driven from its moorings, you are drifting unpiloted on a tempestuous sea. Let these raging waters urge you to take shelter in the alone quiet haven. Oh! if at this season you are *without God!*—a stran-

* "Your mansion above is filling, and your cottage on earth emptying, and what is the language of this dispensation? Onwards, onwards! Upwards, upwards!" — *Helen Plumtre.*

ger to the power of religion—un-
cheered by its precious, gracious
promises, I pity you,—from the
bottom of my heart, I grieve for
you! In the wide world there
is no sadder spectacle than the
poor and unbefriended, the orphaned, or widowed, or withered heart, ungladdened by one
holy beam of Bible consolation!
The dark valley of the Shadow
of Death traversed; and not one
solitary ray falling from the Star
of Bethlehem! Or equally mourn-
ful if the heart be unhumbled—if
it refuse to bear the rod—if the
death chamber only reëcho with
guilty murmurings, and the chast-
ened soul be unable to point to

any "peaceable fruit of righteousness," as the result of the Divine
dealings! There is a depth of
meaning in what a son of consolation has said, as he mingles ex-
hortations with solaces—"unsanctified trials become deep afflictions."

On the other hand, if you are
no stranger to these exceeding
great and precious promises, or
if till now a stranger, you are
ready to avail yourself of this
one only solace in such an hour,
what a hallowed experience yours
is! With all the unutterable, untold depths of your sorrow, I know
not (a *happier* I dare not call it)

but a time fuller of more chasten-
ed joy than the mourning Christian's chamber, when the world
is shut out, and he is *alone with
God !* The sun of his earthly
prosperity set, and set it may be
for ever ! but this only allowing
the bright clustering constella-
tions of Divine consolation to be-
deck the dark firmament ; — the
stars of Bible promise coming out
one by one like ministering angels, and telling of bright scenes
which "eye hath not seen, nor ear
heard, nor heart conceived!" As
in a time of rain and cloud the
distant hills look nearer, so do
the everlasting hills of glory appear, in the cloudy and dark day

nearer, brighter, more glorious,—
sparkling with ten thousand rills
of love and covenant-faithfulness
unseen and unobserved before!
If thus cheered, yours is indeed
an *enviable* lot. The man in the
glitter of worldly prosperity is
not to be envied. But *you* are!
You have got what the world with
all its promises and blandishments
cannot give, and which the world
with all its deceitfulness cannot
take away,—*the Eternal God Himself*, who can fill all blanks, and
compensate for all losses; who
can make that solitary chamber
where you are now mourning
and weeping, a *Patmos*, bright as
the lovely Ægean Isle was to

John, with manifestations of a
Saviour's presence and love.* Remember affliction has always been
God's peculiar method of dealing
with His own people.   It is because He *loves* them He *chastises*
them.   "I have *chosen* thee," says
He, "in the *furnace of affliction.*"
"What son is he whom the Fath-

---

* "If death did come alone to us, it would
be terrible to us indeed, its ghastly countenance would affright us.   But here is the
comfort, that Christ our dearest Lord will
come *with* death to sweeten it to us, and
support us under it.   * *   Though it be the
king of terrors in itself, and a grim porter,
yet by His coming with it, it shall be the
king of comforts." — *John Bunyan.*

"God's ichor fills the hearts that bleed,
  The best fruit loads the broken bough ;
  And in the wounds our sufferings plough
  Immortal love sows sovereign seed."

er chasteneth not?" As an old writer says, "He instructs His scholars in the school of the *Law*, and in the school of the *Gospel*, but He has a third class for advanced learners, and that is the *school of Trial*." A sublime dialogue between a saint on earth and a saint in heaven, represents each member of the white-robed multitude as having graduated in this same school, — "What are these arrayed in white robes, and whence came they? These are they that have come out of *great tribulation*." *

* When Bishop Latimer's landlord informed him that he never knew a trial, "God," was the reply, "cannot be here."

Seek to exercise simple faith in the wisdom of God's dealings, — the unswerving rectitude of His dispensations. He does *all well*, and nothing but what is well. Nothing can come wrong to you that comes from His hand. Confide where you cannot understand. Trust where you cannot trace. Repress all guilty murmurings, check all rebellious thoughts, "Get," as a tried saint expresses it, "your 'hows and whys' crucified, and resolve all into, and rest satisfied in, infinite wisdom tempered with covenant love ; * * He may teach by contraries, but no one teaches like Him." Seek to magnify His name by the sweet

exercise of the grace of *patience.*
This is a grace peculiar to the
saints on earth. It is unknown
in heaven, where there are no
trials to call it into exercise. Glo-
rify God "in the fires." There is
something touchingly beautiful in
the sentiment of Edward Bicker-
steth at his dying hour. "This
day, Saturday, 16th, he called
one of us to him, and directed
this message to his people for
the next day, 'The prayers of
this congregation are desired for
the Rector of this Parish, not that
his life may be spared, but that
he may through his affliction glo-
rify God, by fresh exercises of
faith, patience, and resignation,

and that when the Lord's work
is accomplished he may depart
hence and be with the Lord.'"
Seek, afflicted one, to feel how
light this heavy cross is, in comparison with what your sins de-
served. Ay, and what a drop in
the ocean of suffering it is, in
comparison with what the Prince
of sufferers underwent, whose solitary experience was this,—"ALL
thy waves and thy billows have
gone over me!" He could make
a challenge to a whole world of
sufferers which to this hour re-
mains unanswered, and ever *will*
remain—*Was there ever any sorrow like unto* MY *sorrow?"* Child
of God! if such indeed thou art,

believe it, there is not one drop
of wrath in the bitter cup thou
art now drinking. He took all
that was bitter out of it, and left
it *a cup of love !*

As this your first trial is a new
and never-to-be-forgotten epoch in
your natural life, let it be em-
phatically so in your spiritual.
Hear a voice in it saying, "Arise
and call upon thy God." The
once beaten footroad to the place
of prayer may have been suffer-
ed to be choked up, and covered
with the rank weeds of worldli-
ness and neglect. Let affliction
prove as a sharp sickle, mowing
them down, and once more open-

ing a way to an unfrequented and
deserted mercy-seat. Be it yours
henceforth to rise *above* your trial,
in the only way in which you
would wish to rise above it; viz.
to rise above the world and to
live with God! Let your walk
be close and habitual with Him.
Let your citizenship be in heaven.
A little while and the night of
weeping will be over, and a gen-
tle hand in a tearless world will
dry up the very source of tears.
Oh let this "blessed hope" recon-
cile you to the severest discipline
of earth. Think often of *heaven;*
and that though there be night
(ay, seasons of deepest starless

midnight) *here,* " *there is no night*
THERE." — No bereavement *there*
either to be experienced or dread-
ed! Every day is bringing you
nearer that *home* of joy! nearer
reunion with those glorified, one
of whom, it may be, you are now
mourning; nearer Him who is
now standing with the hoarded
treasures of Eternity in His hand,
and the hoarded love of Eternity
in His heart! How will one brief
moment there, banish in everlasting oblivion all the pangs and
sorrows of the vale of weeping!
"When you have passed," says a
holy man of God who is now
realizing the truth of his own

words, " when you have passed
to the other side of that narrow
river, to the which we shall so
shortly come, you will have no
doubt that all you have under-
gone was little enough for the
desired end."

" Soon and for ever,
  Such promise our trust,
Though ashes to ashes,
  And dust unto dust; —

Soon and for ever
  Our union shall be
Made perfect, our glorious
  Redeemer, in Thee!

When the sins and the sorrows
  Of time shall be o'er,
Its pangs and its partings
  Remembered no more, —

Where life cannot fail,
    And where death cannot sever,
Christians with Christ shall be
    Soon and for ever."

Meanwhile, return to life's duties with the spirit of "a weaned
child," exhibiting meek acquies-
cence in the sovereign will of
your God. Yes! *return to life's
duties!* It is by no means the
smallest part of your trial thus
to go out to breathe the cheerless
air of the world again, and min-.
gle with a saddened and crushed
spirit amid scenes where all is
uncongenial. But impossible as
it may now seem, "the waves of.
life," to use the striking words of

a writer already quoted, "must and will settle back to their usual flow where that treasured bark has gone down. For how imperiously, how coolly, in disregard of all one's feeling, does the hard, cold, uninteresting course of daily realities move on! Still must we eat and drink, and sleep and wake again — still bargain, buy, sell, ask and answer questions—pursue in short a thousand shadows, though all interest in them be over, the cold mechanical habit of living remaining, after all vital interest in it has fled."

But "as thy day, so shall thy strength be." You know not until you make trial of it all the blessed fulness and truthfulness of this precious promise. "You are about," says one deeply experienced, "to enter into realities of consolation you have never imagined to be in God." You have heard ten thousand broken hearts tell in no sembled words what their experience has been. "We have been wonderfully supported." And what was the secret of it? Let a much-tried Apostle answer.—"*All men* forsook me * * Notwithstanding, THE LORD stood by me and strengthened me!" He proportions grace to trial. Your extremity is *His* opportunity. "We went through

the *flood* on foot," says the Psalmist; "THERE did we rejoice in
Him." Beautiful picture of every saint! or rather, glorious tes-
timony to the sustaining grace
of God; a firm footing amid the
threatening waves! — nay more,
"THERE!" (when the billows were
around us; in the very *midst of
our affliction*) — "THERE did we rejoice in Him!" He will deal
tenderly, wisely, lovingly, with
you. God our Maker " giveth
songs in the night." He does not
" pour down waterfloods on the
mown grass." He *considers* His
people's case. " Whatever our
need be, He is below it; underneath are the everlasting arms!"

There is no Bible figure on which the Christian mourner dwells with such delight as that of *the Refiner of silver*, sitting by the furnace of His own lighting — tempering its heat—regulating the fury of the flames — quenching the violence of the fires—designing all, ALL — not to consume and destroy, but to purify, brighten, refine !

I commend you to God and to the word of His grace. I commend you above all to the tenderness of that human sympathy which exists alone in Jesus. Angels and archangels, never having had sorrow, cannot *sympathize*.

The glorious Being before whom
they cast their crowns *can!* for
sorrow tracked *His* footsteps, from
the manger to the grave.*

We never can understand the
depth and preciousness of *His* sympathy until we come to need it.
"I have had a deep, a very deep
wound," says Lady Powerscourt,
"the trial has been very severe,
but how should I have known
Him as a brother born for ad-
versity without it? * * * He
has gone through every class in

* It is striking to note the cases of death
and bereavement which during His ministry
on earth called forth the exalted sympathies
of His human nature, — an *only son!* an *only
daughter!* an *only brother!*

our wilderness-school, He seems
intent to fill up every gap love
has been forced to make. One
of his errands from heaven was,
to bind up the broken-hearted."*
Let your trial only endear Him
to you more and more. Hear
as it were the voice of the departed, stealing down from the
heights of glory, and thus, as
Boaz said to Ruth, gently re-
buking your fast-falling tears,—
"It is true that I am thy near
kinsman, howbeit there is a Kinsman nearer than I!" (Ruth iii.
12.) Though earthly ties have
been severing, He still "lives
and loves." "She was," said good

* *Lady Powerscourt's Letters.*

old Philip Henry, when writing of
Lady Puleston, who died in 1658,
"She was the best friend I had
on earth, but my Friend in heav-
en is still where He was, and He
will never leave me nor forsake
me."*

* "He Himself calls to you with His own
tender, loving voice, 'I am He that was
dead, and behold I am alive for evermore.'
I live *with* thee, my poor afflicted one — I live
for thee — I live *in* thee — I live *with* thee —
never to leave thee by night or by day, in
sickness or in health, in thy drooping morn-
ings or in thy sad evenings, when the heart
faints and the spirits sink, when faith is weak
and nature is strong. — I live *with* thee, to
fill the place of him who is gone, to do that
which no creature can do, and MORE than
fill it, much, much more! — I live *with* thee,
to comfort and to satisfy, yea to sanctify — I
live *with* thee, my child, when every earthly

Go forward to a dark future,
fearlessly relying on His "exceed-

prop sinks and dies. I live *for* thee in heav-
en, to plead thy cause, to communicate grace
from above, grace in every time of need; the
hour, the moment. I live *in* thee, to sustain
thee as thy very life. Such is His sweet
and tender voice, the tender, loving voice of
His own loving heart." — *Evans.*

"Whatsoever, whomsoever you have lost,
you have not lost your Jesus, your best
Friend, your heavenly Husband; you have His
eye, His tender, watchful, provident eye upon
you still, you have His ear open to your
cries still; yea, you have His everlasting arms
underneath you to sustain you still, for else
you would sink. * * To have a friend in
heaven, and such a friend, so wise, so powerful, so faithful, so merciful, so sensibly affect-
ed with all our misery, so tender, so able, and
so willing to bear and help us! — I say this
is infinitely better than all the friends that
ever we had or could have on earth." — *Bunyan Heart's Ease.*

ing great and precious promises."
The future is not yours but His;
He is a rich provider and a wise
provider. Take as your wilder-
ness-watchword, "*I shall not want.*"
He will "guide you (nay, He
is guiding you) by His. counsel,"
"and afterward"—"AFTERWARD!"
—it is not for you or me to
scan that word! It may be
one of painful significance; it
may be *after* much discipline, it
may be *after* a rough and rug-
ged and thorny road; it may be
after trial upon trial, and wave
upon wave. But even on the
darkest and dreariest view of
the future, though this your tri-

al should prove but the com-
mencement of a lengthened "Valley of Baca" (weeping) — one
continuous path of sadness, —
remember what follows that "*afterward*" — "*He will receive you
into Glory!*" Soon the last rip-
ple of sorrow will be heard mur-
muring on the other side of Jor-
dan, and *then* — every vestige
of its sound will die away, and
that *for ever!* Entering the tri-
umphal arch of Heaven, you
will read in living characters the
history of a sinless, sorrowless
future : " And God shall wipe
away all tears from their eyes,
and there shall be no more

death, neither sorrow, nor crying, neither shall there be any
more pain: for the former things
are passed away." Rev. xxi. 4.

"ASK."

Gᴏᴅ's "Ask"
Meaneth all fulness and all grace,
Access in every time and place ;
Yet we
To whom this mercy is so free,
This privilege of light to bask
In the full sunshine of His face,
Regard prayer even as a task.

"GREAT IS THY FAITH."

FAITH is a grasping of Almighty Power;
The hand of man laid on the arm of God;
The grand and blessed hour
In which the things impossible to me
Become the possible, O Lord, through Thee.

"SEEKING REST AND FINDING NONE."

UPON life's troubled sea like waves we toss,
As if there were no God, no Christ, no Cross.
We turn towards the east, towards the west,
Seeking for rest,
Yet finding none.
Light-seekers, shrinking only from the sun,
So we
Refuse the voice to hearken
Of One crying,

In all the agony of love and dying,
    " Come unto Me,"
Until our very light within doth darken.
        It was of rest Christ spoke
When bidding us take up and bear His yoke.

———

WEEP NOT, BELOVED.

" God hath given us eternal life, and this life is in His Son."

WEEP not, beloved:
If God hath called a dear one from thy side,
He lays not on thee more than He hath felt.
    His Son hath died.
    He feels for thee
When thou dost shed a sad, bereavèd tear,
Whose only Son for thy poor sake hath filled
    A human bier.
    And canst thou grudge
To yield to Him thy best-beloved — He
Who gave, in all the fulness of His love,
    His Son for thee ?

LIFE AND DEATH.

" Your sorrow shall be turned into joy."

LIFE and Death drew nigh :
I cried with an exceeding bitter cry,
" Stay thou, O Life ! O Death, pass thou me
     by ! "
Life frowned upon me, but Death gave con-
     sent ;
Yet, pausing ere upon his way he went,
He said, " Thou canst not know what thou
     dost ask."
And from his features he withdrew a mask.
As sunlight shining on a darksome cloud,
Forthwith I saw on his transfigured face
The Shining light of Christ's reflected grace.
     He then drew back
The sombre foldings of his mantle black,
     When in his hands
     A Cross I saw :
" The sceptre which I waved above all lands,
     Striking all hearts with awe,

Christ took from me, and gave me this,
Which I now reach for men to kiss.
Fear not, I only mean thy bliss."
No longer by his hated presence cowed,
I felt that I had judged Death much amiss,
Since not to him, but Christ, we bowed.

THE LIGHT OF LIFE.

" I have yet many things to say unto you, but ye cannot bear them
now."

As one who entereth by night a room
      Where sufferers lie,
Shadeth his lamp to suit the languid eye,
      So doth the Christ draw nigh
      Unto our world of gloom.
The light of life He beareth, and doth stand
Shading it tenderly with piercèd hand,
      Lest the full glare
   Should cause us not to see, but stare.
Yet through the nail-prints some sweet rays
   divine
      Will gently shine :
Dawn which doth for the day prepare.

"HE SHALL SAVE HIS PEOPLE FROM THEIR SINS."

I MET the Saviour in the evening hours,
  The sun was sinking in the quiet west;
His hands were filled with newly-gathered
    flowers,
With which His Father's mansions should be
    dressed.
I looked upon them with a strange surprise;
He read the thought my looks alone expressed:
" Master, are these indeed earth's very best —
Buds, nipped and bitten rudely with the frost;
Blossoms, their petals tempest - torn and
    tossed ?
And surely Thou hast gathered them with
    cost ! "
The Saviour spake with mercy in His eyes:
      " I came to save the lost."
The Son of Man hath healing for His art.
The withering buds men scornfully despise,
God gathers up and freshens on His Heart.

The Gate of Paradise.

*'La mort ne nous séparera pas. Bien loin de là;
. . . J'espère on aime mieux au Ciel où tout se divinise.'—Eugénie de Guèrin.*

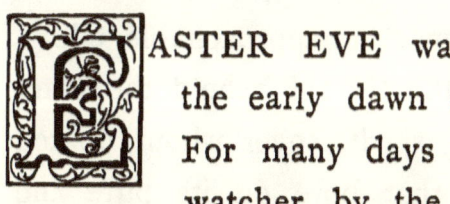ASTER EVE was passing into the early dawn of Easter Day. For many days I had been a watcher by the sick-bed of a dear child; but on this night anxiety had given place to hope, and he had fallen into the deep, serene sleep that foretells returning health.

With a quiet and thankful heart I marked the hours pass, the stars fade in the purple sky, and morning twilight steal over the distant line of gray sea. Even so, I thought, joy eternal 'cometh in the morning;' even so will the last glad Easter dawn, and end the night of all earthly watching.

At length, however, weariness overcame me, and I fell asleep.

And in my dreams I seemed to stand at the Gate of Paradise. Below me were dark clouds and a steep descent; but above me an almost unapproachable Glory. Grouped about the Gate I beheld the forms of many waiting spirits, over whom floated a white banner, that bore on its pure and shining folds a golden Cross surmounted by a Crown.

An angel stood in the entrance, and as I drew near he said, 'Child of Earth, what brings thee to the Land of Light? Speak, and fear not.'

'Truly,' I answered, 'I know neither how nor why I came hither; but I am weak and weary, and if this be Paradise, I pray thee let me in, and cheer me by one sight of its eternal joy.'

The angel smiled.

'Thou art then one of the dreamers of earth,' he said, 'to whom it is at times permitted that while the body sleeps, the soul should for a few brief moments visit the Home of the Blessed. Enter, beloved.'

With these words, he beckoned to one of the fairest of those shining ones I had observed at the Gate, and gave me into her care, saying, 'Gabrielle, take charge of this poor wanderer, and show her such things as she can understand.'

Then Gabrielle took my hand and led me within the gates.

'Thou art surely weary,' she said : 'thou shalt rest beneath the fountain of the water of life.'

So we sat together beneath stately palms that drooped over a clear stream, which, ever flowing from the fountain, took its course by many windings to the sea. And I looked around me, and tried to take in something of the beauty that everywhere met my gaze.

But even as then it far transcended what my utmost thought had conceived, so now words fail me when I would describe that home of the saints.

I can tell of a strange and heavenly light, 'like unto a stone most precious,' that lay in endless glades, and lit up the radiant forms of blessed ones, who, making the air melodious with song, moved to and fro amid groves and plants of unearthly beauty.

I can speak of the 'everlasting hills,' whose outline lay in a golden mist in the far distance, to which Gabrielle pointed as the hills of the Celestial country where the King reigns in perpetual glory. And I can tell of a sea, which, like a belt of molten silver, lies between those shores and Paradise—a sea that knows no storms, and in whose clear deeps I learned can at times be seen, as in a mirror, something of the unknown glories of that New Jerusalem for which the saints in Paradise wait in hope. But I cannot hope to paint in human words the energy of life, the surpassing gladness, the perfection and pure delight, of this land of rest.

On the margin of the stream by which we sat grew many lovely plants; and as they swayed to and fro in the breeze, I thought I could hear amongst their blossoms soft whispers as of prayer. Turning to Gabrielle, I asked if it were so, or if my fancy misled me.

'You are not mistaken,' she said : 'these are the as yet unanswered prayers of some who are still on earth. Stoop, and thou shalt hear.'

Then I bent over a fair lily, and in its pure chalice heard, as it were, a distant echo of these words : 'Lord, he hath lost the faith and love of his childhood— he hath wandered from Thee and from me : bring him home at last!' 'Alas,' I said, 'surely this is the prayer of a mother for her son!'

Again I listened, and from the crimson bell of another flower I heard—'Lord! that I might receive my sight.' And I said 'Amen ;' for at that moment it seemed as though I could not bear that blind man's cross.

Once more I leant over those strange

blossoms, and my ear caught these sounds, uttered with a clearer, intenser cry than either of the other petitions—'O God, if indeed Thou art anywhere in space, teach me where to find Thee; teach me how to believe on Thee!'

But even as I listened, the words died away, the flower closed its petals, drooped, and then passed from my sight, leaving in its stead a radiant jewel, on which was graven some word I could not read.

Then Gabrielle's countenance shone with a new glory. 'Praised be our God,' she said, 'who hath at length heard the voice that cried unto Him out of the darkness.' She then told me that this jewel would be treasured up for the crown of the suppliant at the Day of Resurrection; and at that moment an angel passed by, who gathered it, with other gems from amongst the flowers, and bore it away in his golden basket.

Then I asked of my guide if sooner or later all these prayers would receive an answer.

'Not so,' she replied. 'The prayer of faith is not always a prayer of knowledge—though, being the token of faith and love, it is most dear to the King. Yet be thou not discouraged. The continual intercession of the saints on earth ever receiveth acceptance and answer, though it may be after long waiting. Pray therefore night and day for those thou lovest: thou wilt not pray in vain.'

Then she took me aside where other flowers grew, whose blossoms were of such marvellous and dazzling whiteness that I could scarcely look upon them; but it seemed to me that they were marked with blood.

' Touch them not,' she said; ' but kneel and listen, if perchance thou mayest hear the voice of these.'

And I knelt upon the ground, and heard —'O My Father, if it be possible, let this cup pass from Me: nevertheless, not as I will, but as Thou wilt.'

Awed and wondering, I looked at Gabrielle for an explanation; but she only said gently, ' For thy sake and for mine was this prayer unheard.'

We wandered on until we came to a bed of strangely fantastic creepers. ' These,' said my guide, ' are the delight of the Prince when He comes among us: they are the unanswered prayers of little children. Strangely sweet they are, and full of faith; but often such as if granted would bring no true joy to the little ones.'

' What then become of their flowers? ' I asked; and she replied that the Prince loved them, and that He would often gather and place them in His bosom, for He had said there was no sound in Heaven or earth so sweet as the prayer of a little child.

Here also I perceived many a gem half hidden by the quivering leaves until the Angel should pass that way with his gathered jewels.

Just then a dove, whose soft plumage gleamed like burnished silver, alighted on Gabrielle's shoulder. 'Sing me thy song, bright one,' she said as she took it on her hand. And the bird leaned his head caressingly against her cheek, and sang. And underneath the melody of his singing I seemed to hear the glad burden of the song of some rejoicing soul: 'Weeping may endure for a night; but joy cometh in the morning.'

'And now thou seest,' continued Gabri-

elle, 'that every living thing, every leaf
and blossom in Paradise, hath a voice of
praise or prayer; and so strangely yet truly
are we linked to the saints on earth, that
the very sounds of their supplication or of
their joy finds here an echo.'

We now perceived four lovely maidens
approaching us, who from their resemblance
to one another I took to be sisters. They
were evidently full of some new cause for
gladness, and as they drew near we heard
their joyous voices. 'Gabrielle, beloved,
be glad with us,' said one of them. 'She
is coming at last. Even now is the Angel on his way to fetch her, and we go
to the Gate to receive her. Think you
she will know us again?'

'Aye, truly, sweet one,' said Gabrielle.
'Surely, through earth or Heaven a mother
will know her own!'

They passed on quickly to the Gate,

and I saw them no more: but my heart rejoiced as I thought of the meeting again of those long parted ones.

' Thou art, then, a mother?' I asked of my fair companion, whose earnest reply had struck me.

'My husband and child are still upon earth,' she answered. 'When the Master called me hither, I seemed to have much to leave; and yet, I know not how it was, but when I heard His Voice my soul rose up hastily, like blessed Mary, and went out gladly to meet Him. And now, she continued, 'I find it was to add the love and joy of Paradise to the love and gladness of earth. We are still one, though parted; and the time is short.'

'And hast thou seen them since that sad hour of parting?' I asked.

'Aye,' she replied; 'twice hath the Prince sent me to earth. Once it was to save

my little one from a horrible death. I
found her playing on the brink of a hidden
well; and I took her back to those who,
in sorrow and fear, were vainly seeking
her.'

'Did they see thee?' I asked.

'The child saw me; and when she spoke
of it, they went forth to seek me, and
knew not that I stood beside them. So I
returned again to await them here. And
once again I visited earth. When in his
loneliness my husband's prayer came up,
saying, that since the Lord had set the
cross of suffering on his path, henceforth
life should be to him one continued service, and offering himself as one who
would carry the name of Christ into perilous and heathen lands; then, on the
night on which he sailed, as he lay asleep
in the ship, the Master sent me to bid
him be of good cheer. I know not if

in his dreams he saw me; but when I
spoke he smiled, and I heard him murmur
" Gabrielle," and then—"Christ." '

'And is this long ago?' I asked.

'Nay, I cannot tell,' she said, smiling;
'for the time is ever short in Paradise.'

And now a very wondrous though distant burst of melody filled the air, unlike
any sound that I had heard; but so joyous, so pervading, so perfect was the har-
mony, that I earnestly asked from whence
it came.

'It is indeed a blessed sound,' said Gabrielle. 'It is borne on heavenly gales from
the celestial country: in a moment it will
be taken up, and echoed back by every
dweller in Paradise, for to us also it is a
sound of joy. It is the song of the Angels in the Presence of God over some
sinner that repenteth.'

'Ah!' I thought, 'if it might but be the

son for whom that mother prayed, whose prayer breathed in the lily!'

Divining my wish, Gabrielle turned, and we retraced our steps to the margin of the stream; and there, where the fair lily had been, lay a glorious opal, casting back from its polished surface the many-tinted lights of Paradise. Then we knew that the mother's prayer was heard.

And now I asked my guide to speak to me concerning the Prince.

'Does He come often among you?'

'So often,' she replied, 'that we seem to be ever in His Presence. Even now look toward the sea, for I think I behold His beloved form crossing from the other side. Let us go forth to meet Him.'

It was even so. The air rang with songs of welcome, and glittered with countless radiant spirits, who formed in shining ranks to receive their Lord, as, walking royally on the unruffled surface of the waters, He passed over from the celestial shore.

Then, as He approached, I trembled exceedingly, and fell to the ground, that I might not look upon the Divine Majesty of His Presence.

When I raised my eyes He was gone; but an angel stood beside us, and was speaking to my companion in these words:

'Gabrielle, beloved, rejoice! for I am sent to thee on a glad errand. This night must thy husband finish his course on earth. "Go thou," saith the Master, "stand by him in the last conflict, and bring him hither to eternal joy!"'

On this Gabrielle bowed her head and worshipped. 'So soon,' I heard her murmur—'so soon! So brief a parting—so eternal a reunion!'

'True,' replied the angel; 'yet can I bear witness that to him the time has seemed long. Twenty of earth's years has he labored in the wilderness since thou wert taken from him—aye,' he added fervently, 'labored and hath not fainted.'

At these words Gabrielle raised her eyes, and by the look of glad surprise that filled them, I saw that to her it had seemed but as a summer's day since she too had been a worker on earth.

'Let me go!' she said eagerly; 'but would that I might also look on the face of my child!'

'Do even as thou wilt,' replied the Angel; 'and the merciful guiding of the Most High be with thee!'

With these words he passed on; and Gabrielle, in the glow of her beauty and her joy, sprang toward the Gate.

But I cried after her, 'O Gabrielle! take

me back to earth, for I am weak, and the glory of Paradise lies like a weight upon my spirit!'

With a compassionate smile she once more took my hand, and we passed out together. And soon the light of that golden land glimmered like a distant star behind us, and we no longer heard the songs of the dwellers there.

When we reached earth, I saw that we stood beneath the shadow of an old church. It was night; but I could see how peaceful a resting-place it was for the dead. Round many of the graves flowering plants were blossoming; and an avenue of limes veiled them tenderly with a network of soft shadows. We stood by a cross of marble, that gleamed like snow in the moonlight. It bore the simple inscription :

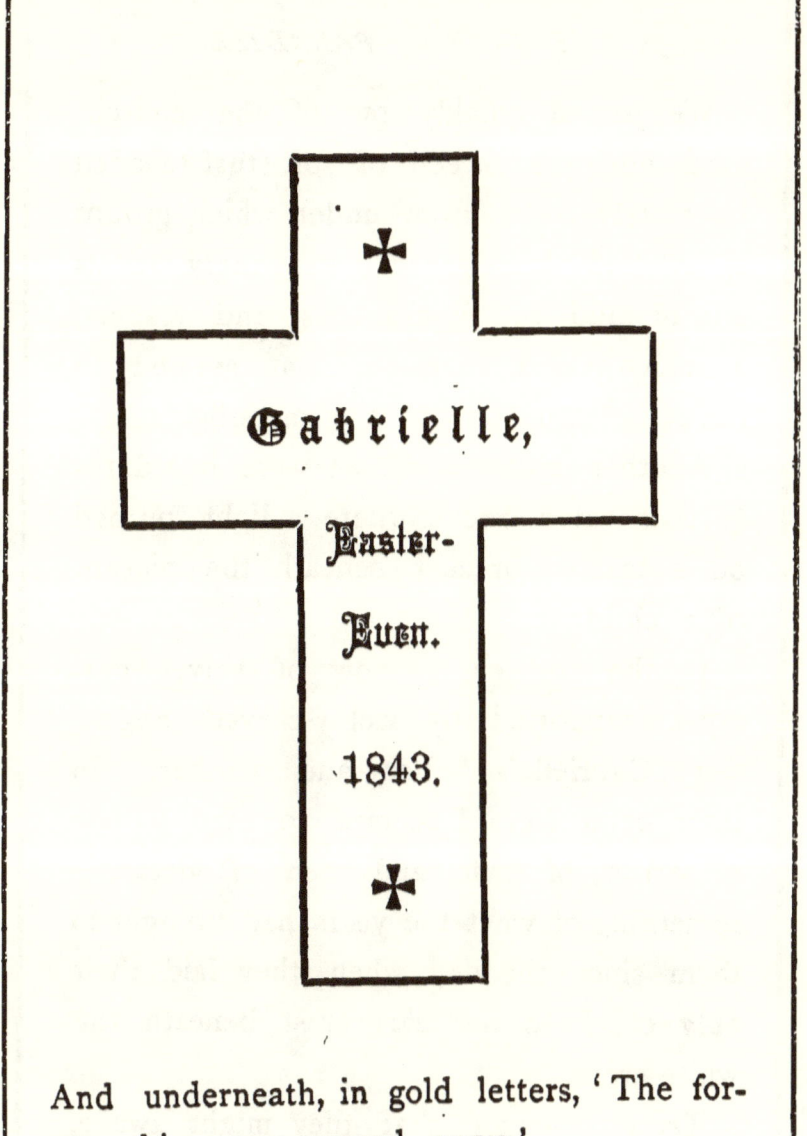

Gabrielle,

Easter-

Even.

1843.

And underneath, in gold letters, ' The former things are passed away.'

We passed quickly out of the church-
yard, on to a sweep of soft turf shaded
by stately trees, from under which groups
of startled deer gazed wonderingly at us
out of mild and liquid eyes, and reached
a many-gabled mansion, that seemed to
lie in solemn state in the moonlight.

Another moment, and we were in a dark-
ly wainscoted room, where a light burned
on a marble bracket beneath the picture
of a child.

In the crimson shadow of velvet cur-
tains, supported by richly-carved angels,
slept Gabrielle's father and mother. In
their calm faces I seemed to read a tale
of sorrow, of strife, and then of victory—
something of what the years had brought to
them since the day when they laid their
only child to her early rest beneath the
white cross.

Truly I longed that they might awake,

if but for one moment, to behold their darling as she bent over them—the deep pure love of Heaven shining in that steadfast gaze. But they lay in so majestic a repose, that I could almost fancy them the marble effigies on some ancient tomb.

And now Gabrielle led the way to an inner room, where a fair girl lay asleep. So very fair was she, so like to the bright spirit at her side, as she lay with her golden hair about her pillow—'like a saint's glory up in Heaven'—that I needed not to ask if this were Gabrielle's child.

It was evident that she had fallen asleep with happy thoughts, for a smile was on her lip, and in her hand she held a letter, with which even in her slumbers she seemed unable to part. Her finger lay on these words:—'Beloved child, this is no place for thee; yet if they need thee not, and thou hast so resolved, I dare not keep thee from thy crown. The harvest truly is great, and the laborers are few.—Come.'

'Nay, my treasure,' said Gabrielle, reading the words as she bent fondly over her child. 'The Lord hath need of thee here, not in heathen lands; and the Lord hath need of thy father, but not upon earth. Farewell! In comforting others shalt thou be comforted; in strengthening others shalt thou find strength; in loving shalt thou be loved. Fare thee well!'

In another moment we were again in the cool night air, passing swiftly southward. At times I heard far below us the murmur of the sea, or saw the glittering lights of strange cities, or caught the sound of some heathen revel, or the howl of some unsatisfied beast of prey.

At length we came to the borders of a dense forest. A humble spire rose from a group of neatly built huts and cultivated gardens, which contrasted strangely with the wilderness around; and I saw that it was a Christian village in the midst of a heathen land.

'This way,' said Gabrielle suddenly. 'Surely I heard him call me!' And she led me into a low hut.

On a rude shelf in the wall a lamp was burning with a dull flare; and the light fell on the dusky faces and white dress of two native servants. One sat on the ground, rocking himself to and fro in a despair that was sorrowful to behold; while the other strove vainly to stanch a terrible spear-wound in his master's side, from which the life-blood was slowly oozing.

On a rough pallet beneath the lamp lay Anselm, Gabrielle's husband. His eyes were closed, and he appeared unconscious. Then Gabrielle knelt beside him, and I saw her throw her arms about him, and call him by every tender name; but he only groaned heavily.

And now, for the first time, I saw standing on the other side an angel whose presence made me tremble, so terrible a light was in his eye, so hard and unsparing the curve of lip and brow. With a low voice, that yet seemed to ring through the hut and arouse the dying man, he spoke: 'To what end hast thou labored these twenty years? Hath God indeed acknowledged thy work? Hath He not crossed thy life with anguish, read thy prayers backward, forsaken thee, and left thee to die like a dog by the hand of a miserable heathen? Curse Him, for thou canst but die!'

Then the dying priest groaned again; and I thought I heard him murmur, 'Forsake me not when my strength faileth.'

In vain Gabrielle tried to interpose between her beloved and the angel of dark-

ness. The soft tones of her spirit voice
seemed to awake no response in the ear
of the dying man; and the evil one, with
a mocking laugh, continued his derisive
words. Then I saw the shadow of a human agony pass into her glorious eyes:
yet only for a moment, for, looking up to
Heaven, I heard her breathe the words,
'My Saviour! I am but a weak spirit, but
Thou art God!' And in an instant a soft
light filled the room, and He on Whom
she called stood by His fainting servant.
I saw Him lay a Hand, marked even then
with the print of the nail, on Anselm's
brow, where the damps of death were fast
gathering; and I saw that the dying man
had returned to consciousness, for he mur-
mured, 'Thanks be to God, Who giveth
us the victory through our Lord Jesus
Christ;' and then the light faded, and I
saw the Divine Master no more.

But I knew that the end was come; for Gabrielle stood beside her husband, and he knew her, and was stretching out his arms toward her, and the joy of Paradise was in both their faces.

And now the wretched lamp flickered for the last time, and went out. In the darkness I heard a long-drawn sigh; and when I looked again, the moonlight was streaming in at the open door on the white features of the dead.

For a moment Anselm and Gabrielle stood together by the pale corpse, and then, for the first time, I marked how strangely alike they were. In the solemn hush of that moment, the newly-disembodied soul seemed to pause, as one on the threshold of a mighty destiny. The countenance told of Faith, that was even then almost sight, of strength blended with profoundest humility, and by the visible

expression of these I recognized Anselm;
while by the matchless tenderness, the radiant joy that illuminated the other—joy as
of one in full and conscious possession of
supreme and perpetual bliss—I could not
fail to distinguish Gabrielle.   Was it that
by diverse methods perfection had been
wrought in each?—that what joy had accomplished in one had been effected by
stern griefs in the other?—or that both
spirits had been cast in one mould by
the Great Master of Life?

I know not: but while I thought on these
mysteries of life and death, a wail of sorrow rose from the faithful servants as Gabrielle and Anselm passed out into the
night; and the last I heard of them was
the exulting voice of Gabrielle beneath the
stars, singing 'Home! home!'

And I?—I awoke from my dream to find
a small wasted hand placed in mine, and a
weak voice singing in low tones of quiet
content, the last verse of the hymn with
which we had lately beguiled the weary
night:

> ' O Paradise ! O Paradise !
> I know 'twill not be long !
> Patience—I almost think I hear
> Faint fragment of thy song.
> Where loyal hearts and true
> Stand ever in the light ;
> All rapture through and through
> In God's most Holy sight ! '

It may be that the child's voice had
blended with my dreams; that his hand,
not Gabrielle's, had led me through strange
paths, and that the glorious Easter sunshine that filled the room had suggested
the light of Paradise.

It may be so: but still it seems to me

that when this life is over, and my weary
soul, borne by some blessed angel, is carried within the golden gates, I may yet see
Gabrielle and Anselm standing together
beneath the drooping palms.

www.ingramcontent.com/pod-product-compliance
Lightning Source LLC
Chambersburg PA
CBHW032146010726
47493CB00008BA/2596